TIMEFLIES

THE MAIDEN VOYAGE

M.C. GOLDRICK

For Hannah,
I hope you enjoy
the adventure!

MG

D1292364

TIMEFLIES:

THE MAIDEN VOYAGE

BOOK #1 OF THE TIMEFLIES SERIES

Text copyright © 2018 by M.C. Goldrick

ISBN 978-1-7752231-0-8

MotherButterfly Books

For Dean, Bennett, Caitlin and Felix with love.
It's my great pleasure, privilege and honour to live life with
you. Thank you for being you.

CONTENTS

BONUS MATERIALS

1

AGREE TO AGREE

MY NAME IS GRIZELDA DAY. Yes, Grizelda, not a name you often hear outside fairy tales. I am 9 years old, live in Ottawa, Ontario, Canada and recently, after my friend Alisha and I were trying to understand why my parents had chosen such a bizarre name, something happened. Something extraordinary, something nothing short of amazing.

So, why were we trying to figure it out? Why couldn't we ask them? Perhaps my folks are dead or living in an asylum for the criminally insane. Nope. They're just busy. Most of my questions are met with a distracted "Hmm?", or on a good day, "We'll talk about that later." But later never comes.

They're always in a rush. In the morning, while they're running late for work, I get myself out the door to catch the bus. After school, I walk to my best friend Alisha Summers' house.

They often work late, then they're busy making dinner and cleaning up. We have some time together before bedtime, but they are mostly distracted by their phones. When I try to talk with them, they are always asking me to hold on while they answer an email or reply to a text. If I had my own phone I could text them my questions; still, I doubt they'd actually respond.

So, we had to discover on our own how I came to bear a name typically reserved for storybook stepsisters. That was our first question the day we became TIMEFLIES. But I'm getting ahead of myself. To explain, I'll start at the beginning.

It was a Friday evening, and I was at Alisha's house. We were discussing my mysterious name, when her brother, Sam, bounded in holding a shimmering gold pouch.

Sam is a year older and always cracking jokes, keeping us in stitches. Sam and Alisha's mom watches me after school, so the three of us hang out every day. I consider him my surrogate brother and he calls me Alisha's twin.

He listened as we contemplated their name choice. Then, with a mischievous smile, he asked, "Wouldn't you love to be a fly on the wall?"

Alisha looked intrigued and I wondered, *What's he up to now?*

"I've got just the thing to know everything," he declared, swinging the bag.

"What'dya got?" Alisha ran over, ready to snatch it from his hand.

"Hold your horses!" He lifted it high above his head. "Before I open it, you both have to agree."

"Agree?" I asked. Sam is always planning something.

Some of those things are awesome fun, others, a major pain.

"Well, I had to agree when I bought these," he said.

"Agree to what?" asked Alisha, making a renewed attempt to grab the bag. Sam leaped onto the couch, stretching to keep it out of reach.

"I had to agree to only share with those who agree. So, do you agree?"

"Oh fine, I agree," she conceded, giving up on getting the bag from her taller brother. "My curiosity wins, I'm willing to risk it. Gimme!"

Sam looked at me expectantly. "Well Griz, what about you? Are you in or what?"

"How can I agree to something when I don't even know what I'm agreeing to?" I asked.

"How can I tell you something I'm only allowed to tell people who agree until you agree?"

"Wow, that throws logic right out the window," was all I could say. Sometimes the way he thinks makes my head spin.

"Come on Griz, agree. It's got to be something good," Alisha pleaded. "Look at that bag. It's *gold*," she said, emphasizing gold in a low dramatic tone.

I laughed and snorted loudly, which made us all laugh. "All right, I'm game. What's in the mysterious golden bag?"

Sam put on a serious expression. "You have to agree," he said, twitching as he tried to suppress a smirk.

"I agree," I replied, exasperated.

Breaking out into a grin that filled his whole face, eyes, and eyebrows too, Sam yipped in delight and plopped onto the couch. "Woot woot! The Griz is in! I'm so psyched! This will be epic."

"Open the bag already!" Alisha made a lunging motion, grabbing the bag.

"OK, I will," he said, shaking off his sister's grip and reaching inside the bag. "But prepare yourselves for the adventure of a lifetime." I rolled my eyes. Little did I know how right he was.

LITTLE AMBER CUBES

REACHING INTO THE BAG, Sam retrieved three amber cubes. Each had something small and black suspended within. We huddled for a better view.

"What are those?" I asked. "Flies?"

Lifting a cube, Alisha peered inside. "Yep, they're flies."

"Sam, are these novelty bug candies?" I asked.

Not waiting for an answer, I kept going. There was no way I'd eat bugs, and I was not going to be shy about it.

"Because, if this is your adventure, I don't care if I agreed, it's not happening. I'm a vegetarian for starters and even if I ate animals, I'd still skip the bugs."

"Ah, don't worry," he replied to my rant, "You don't eat them anyway, one lick is enough."

"Enough for what?" Alisha asked.

Sniffing the cube, she wrinkled her nose in disgust and dropped it back into Sam's hand. "Enough to make you sick? Lose your lunch? I'm with Griz. They're all yours, Sam."

"They're not *supposed* to taste good," he replied, frustration creeping into his voice.

"Candy with flies is pushing it, but candy that isn't supposed to taste good, what's the point of that?" I asked.

"It's not candy!" he shouted.

"Well, if it isn't candy then what is it? You said we're supposed to lick it, right?" Alisha asked.

Trying to calm himself, he took a deep breath, "If you two would stop talking for one minute, I could explain," he said.

"OK, fine." I said, looking at my watch, "I'll give you two minutes. Go."

"Drumroll please," said Sam. He was just about to begin, when Mrs. Summers walked in. Sam slipped the cubes back into the bag, discreetly hiding it behind his back.

"Kids, it's time for dinner. Go wash up," she said.

I was eating dinner at their house, again. Another night my parents worked late.

"You got it big momma. We'll be right in," Sam replied with a grin.

After she left the room, Alisha turned to Sam. "Is this something to hide from Mom?" she asked, motioning towards the bag.

"Absolutely. You'll understand better once I've explained. Also, two minutes will not cut it. I'll tell you after dinner, promise."

We had no choice but to wait. With our minds occupied by Sam's forthcoming explanation, we had little to say, leaving the conversation to the adults. Dinner felt *very* long.

Finishing the last bites of lasagna, I pushed my salad around my plate so it would appear as though I had eaten more.

"Well, you kids are quiet this evening," commented their dad. "It's nice for a change," he said, chuckling at his dad joke. "No seriously, tell us about your day."

As Alisha related mundane details, my mind wandered. My curiosity was piqued, I thought, *What's so special about those cubes?*

Unwilling to wait longer, I gobbled my dessert to return to our conversation. My mouth was full of peach cobbler and ice cream when the doorbell rang. Darn, it was my dad, of all the days to show up early. Well, earlier.

Dad chatted as I gathered my things. Though he and my mother made little time to talk to me, he always had a lot to say to other people. At the door, I said goodbye, promising to visit the next day.

"Actually Grizelda, you won't be seeing your friends until Monday. Your mother and I have a surprise for you. We're taking you to Toronto this weekend."

My heart sank. Shooting Sam and Alisha a regretful

look, I forced a fake smile, turned to my dad, and with phony enthusiasm said, "Great."

I left their house knowing Sam would soon tell Alisha about the mysterious cubes. I didn't expect them to wait all weekend, but I did wish, and not for the first time, that I was a Summers.

3

WHAT A TRIP

TORONTO WAS NICE. Well, the city was. It's a beautiful place with much to offer. We did a lot of things there— me, my parents and their phones.

At the zoo, with their eyes locked on screens, they viewed the animals through the camera's lens.

In the CN Tower, we posed for pictures, smiling with the skyline at our backs. While they tweeted and Face-booked about the fun we were having, I, alone, took in the view. So many buildings, streets, and cars, stretching as far as the eye could see. So many people, surrounding me in every direction. Yet, I felt isolated and alone.

We had lunch at a restaurant where we ate in relative silence as they caught up on the news. I exchanged more words with the waiter than I did my parents.

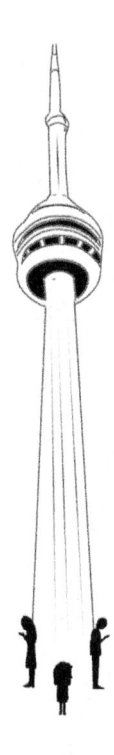

At the hotel pool, while my dad sat in a lounger staring at his laptop, I swam alone. Grimly, I wondered if he'd even notice if I drowned. After ordering room service, we watched separate movies on separate iPads before falling asleep.

The next morning at brunch, I broke the silence by asking them why they had named me Grizelda.

"Hmm?" my mom murmured, absorbed in her phone.

"Well, it's a rather unusual name and not just for someone my age. What made you choose it?"

"Grizelda was your mother's choice," my dad said. "We made a deal, if you were a boy I picked the name. A girl, and your mother got to choose. Grizelda's a great name. But my names were even better, you could have been Slash or Axel, in honour of my favourite band."

My mother still hadn't looked up. I wasn't sure if she was zoned out or didn't want to answer. Her lack of response was unsurprising, pretty much what I had expected. I didn't feel like pushing the issue and assumed there was someone in a rock band named Grizelda.

~

Monday, at school, Alisha nearly bowled me over in class. "Oh Griz, you won't believe what those cubes do. Well, I'm not totally sure I believe it, but we agreed to wait for you. We'd never travel without you. I mean, if they work... but I sure hope they do."

Before I could find out more, the teacher clapped, "Students, please have a seat. Grizelda, you and Alisha can resume your conversation at recess."

Waiting for the bell to sound, I heard each second tick by. The clock, a background metronome, keeping time as Alisha's words echoed in my head. *Never travel without you?* I'm the one who had travelled—what did she mean?

As we left class, Alisha grabbed my hand. I ran to keep up as she dragged me across the yard and out of earshot.

"Time travel, Griz. It's time travel." My head spun. *Was she serious?* I wondered to myself.

"You lick the cube and time travel? Is that what you're saying?" I asked, my voice reflecting my incredulity.

"Yes. That's what the guy who sold them to Sam promised."

"Did he have magic beans too? Come on Lish, you

don't really think they'll work? Clearly, Sam's been swindled."

"Do you think? Oh, I hope not, I really want to time travel," Alisha whined.

Poor gullible Sam, I wondered how much he had spent on useless candies. He had just turned ten, it was probably all of his birthday money. I felt bad for him. I decided, then and there, to go along with it, to have fun pretending, to try to get lost in the make-believe.

"Well, maybe not," I conceded. "Maybe they'll work."

Alisha brightened up, "Only one way to find out. Here comes Sam, let's give it a try."

Seeing Sam bounding towards us, galloping with a ginormous smile, made me glad I decided to play along. "So, did you tell her?" he asked.

"I did," Alisha replied.

"Yay, time travel, super cool." I gave him a double thumbs up.

He nodded, his shaggy hair bouncing "I know, right?"

"I didn't give her the details, haven't had a chance," Alisha said.

"Oh, the details?" I asked, "You mean like how you set the time period you travel to?"

"Yeah, kinda, you might think it's a little strange, though," Alisha replied.

Stranger than licking a candy with a fly inside and travelling through time? I thought. Instead, I said, "Try me, I'll keep an open mind."

Alisha looked to Sam, who, as the expert on this make-believe subject, jumped in to explain. "You ask a question, you lick the cube and close your eyes. When you open them, you're at the place and time that holds the answer to that question. Past, present or future. You observe the surrounding environment to get the answer. Also, you're a housefly."

"A fly? Of course," I said, trying to keep a straight face. "Yes, the fly in the cube, makes perfect sense." It did not. But I was trying to be supportive, right?

"Tell her how we get back," Alisha said.

"There are two ways. One, is you get the answer to your question and you're back to human. The other, is you die. Not *you*, you—but the fly you," he said.

"Huh?" This was getting even crazier. "You die?"

"Yup, the fly dies and boom, you're back to the moment you left, no time has passed. A housefly's average lifespan is between 15-30 days, that's how long we get to figure out the answer. So, unless you get swatted or something, you could have about a month to explore. To see whatever there is to see," Sam explained.

"It doesn't hurt though, you just pop back into you," Alisha added, snapping her fingers for emphasis.

I wanted to play along, but this was ridiculous. I wasn't sure I could hold back any longer. Afraid my voice would betray my misgivings, I nodded and smiled.

"After you left, we were dying to try it out, but we wouldn't go without you," said Alisha.

"It was hard, but we waited for you," Sam added. "Instead, we made a list."

"A list?" I asked.

"Yes, a list of questions, things to ask. They have to be about someone in your family. You can't just ask about dinosaurs and show up in the Jurassic era or John A. Macdonald and show up in 1867 Parliament," Sam explained.

"Unless he's one of our great, great, great grandfathers or something. It only works if you're related," said Alisha.

"We put your question at the top of the list, we thought since you were talking about it when I came home, it could be our first trip," said Sam.

"What question? I forget what we were talking about," I admitted.

"About your name, why your parents named you Grizelda," Alisha said.

"Oh yeah, that. I asked them this weekend."

"You did, well don't hold out on us girl, what did they tell you?" Sam asked.

"Nothing really. My dad said it was my mom's choice, that if I was born a girl she got to choose the name. She didn't tell me anything—acted like she hadn't heard the question."

"Well then, are you ready to find out?" asked Alisha, bouncing on her heels.

"Right now? At school?" I asked. It seemed like an inopportune time.

"It doesn't matter where we are when we try it. We return to the exact moment we left, no one will notice. So, are you good to go?" asked Alisha.

"Sure," I replied. I didn't think this would work, so it didn't matter when we did it or what question we asked. *Let's get this charade over with,* I thought, as Sam handed out the cubes.

Clearing his throat, in a gruff old man voice that was likely supposed to be a wizard, Sam said, "Repeat after me. Oh, fly cube, show us the answer to our question: How did Grizelda Day's mother choose her name?"

He and Alisha held up their cubes and looked at me. I

reluctantly lifted mine. Together, we repeated in unison, "Oh, fly cube, show us the answer to our question: How did Grizelda Day's mother choose her name?"

We closed our eyes and licked our cubes, which did not taste like candy, but vinegar, blue cheese, and dirt.

As I'd predicted, nothing seemed to happen. Suppressing my self-righteousness, I instead chose to commiserate with my friends' disappointment. I opened my eyes, ready to console them, but they were gone. At least, I thought they were. All I saw before me were two tiny houseflies.

4

FLYING HIGH

SHOCKED, I tried to blink, but I had no eyelids. The intensity of the light surrounding me had a peculiar reflective glare. I could see peripherally, simultaneously taking in the view in front, and on both sides. What I could see of my body was black, and, well, the body of a fly. Yes, for all my misgivings, I was a fly.

Being very nearsighted, everything, but the flies before me, was a blur. I assumed the two flies were Sam and Alisha and their comically high-pitched buzzing voices confirmed my theory. This might have made me laugh, but I was struggling not to cry.

"Woah, cool," said, what I took to be, the Sam fly.

"It worked, it worked," said, what I assumed, was the Alisha fly.

Freaking out, not ready to hear my own fly voice, I said nothing. I was not prepared for this. I thought we'd lick the cubes, I'd console Sam for foolishly wasting his money, the recess bell would ring and we'd return to class. End of story. Instead, it was the beginning of a story —the story of our adventures as TIMEFLIES.

The Sam fly lifted off and took flight. "I can fly," he buzzed. "Griz, Lish, try it. It's awesome," he said, confirming his identity.

Alisha, jumped up once and landed back on her little fly feet. "Flap your wings," called Sam, zigzagging above us.

"Oh yeah, wings." She jumped again, this time batting her wings.

"This is wonderful! C'mon Griz, come fly with us," she whirred, hovering beside her brother.

I couldn't do it. I couldn't jump up and fly with them. I was terrified. This didn't feel fun; it was a nightmare. I didn't want to be a fly. I would not have licked that cube had I thought it would work.

Whimpering like an electronic toy with a fading battery, though no tears formed in my weird insect eyes, I wept.

I tried to cover my face with my little black stick hands but they were too narrow. Desperate, I looked around. There was a giant pile of newspapers to my right. Well, they were regular sized—only giant compared to me. I scurried underneath a loose page, hiding myself from view.

"Griz, where are you going? Don't your wings work?" asked Sam. I was beginning to recognize his voice within the buzzing.

"Is something wrong?" asked Alisha, landing nearby.

"I AM A FLY!" I screamed in my tiny voice.

"So are we," she replied in as soothing a tone as a fly

girl can manage, "It's OK. Remember, we licked the cubes. We knew this would happen."

"No, *I* didn't know this would happen!" I cried. "*I* thought this *wouldn't* happen! I thought you were out of your minds thinking this was real!"

Sam and Alisha exchanged a look, surprised, I assume, by my reaction. But without being able to read their facial features, I could only guess.

"You didn't believe us?" asked Sam.

"Sorry, but no, I didn't," I replied.

"Then why did you go along with it? Why didn't you say something?" asked Alisha.

"I love you guys. I didn't want to hurt your feelings. Plus, I thought Sam had wasted his birthday money on a scam. I figured you'd find out soon enough," I explained.

"Aw, you love us, we love you too." Alisha bounded over to give me an awkward fly version of an embrace.

Sam landed, "Best money I ever spent! Thanks for trying to protect my feelings, but it worked. It worked! We're flies. We're TIMEFLIES!"

Barreling over, he inserted himself into our circle. Turning it into a group hug threw off our balance, and we tumbled over buzzing with laughter. Though this was unexpected, now that I was here I decided to make the most of it. I had the chance to experience life as a real fly with my two closest friends. This could be fun.

With that in mind, I set to batting my wings. It was easy, almost effortless. I simply thought of it and it happened. Even though I was new to this form, my body had an innate sense of how to move. An inner knowing of how to operate. It wasn't like learning to fly a plane.

There were no controls to figure out, there was no learning curve. We merely thought of where we wanted to go and an automatic physical response kicked in.

I hovered above my friends, who sat below me. Were they smiling? Hard to tell, but they were definitely delighted that I was on board. They began hooting and hollering, one of them inaudibly clapping their little fly hands in appreciation.

"I'm glad it worked, thanks for sharing your birthday money with us, Sam," I shouted. "Come on, let's take these fly wings out for a spin."

Together, we took off through the air, moving at a fast clip, building momentum until we reached our top speed. Though we were in a room of ordinary size, in relation to us, it seemed huge. We could turn swiftly. As we approached a wall, we could shift to the left or right effortlessly.

We circled around the room, sailing over fixtures, ducking under tables, weaving around obstacles. Like a trio of fighter jets performing complex aerial manoeuvres, we each took a turn at the front, setting the pace and direction, while the other two rode behind in formation.

We were in a kitchen. Being nearsighted and tiny in relation to the surrounding objects, this had not been immediately apparent. I did not recognize the common kitchen appliances until getting closer to them. Olive green instead of the pervasive stainless steel of 2018, they were not the modern versions to which I was accustomed. The tattered walls bore faded wallpaper. The counters were cracked, and worn wood cupboard doors hung lopsidedly from rusted hinges. Disordered and cluttered, empty bottles and dirty dishes covered every surface in the gloomy kitchen.

As we descended to land, a dull light shone meekly through a filmy frosted window, illuminating Sam and Alisha's iridescent bodies. Touching down in the kitchen sink, we landed beside a leaky faucet dripping onto a mound of dirty plates. Thirsty from all that flying, the beaded drops of water were tempting.

Though I felt weird about drinking off a filthy plate, I reminded myself that for the time being I was a fly and went for it. The water was cool and refreshing. I had barely made a dent in the bead when my thirst was fully quenched.

"Where do you think we are, Griz? Anything look familiar here?" Sam asked.

"I have no idea. Clearly it's a kitchen, and either it's very dated or we did go back in time," I replied.

"I wonder how far back," Alisha mused. "I know—let's go check those newspapers you hid under."

"Great idea," I said, impressed by her ingenuity. Alisha was always coming up with creative solutions.

We flew back to the table and landed on the stack of papers. Alisha read the date aloud, "Jan 29, 1983, and look, I don't think we're in Ottawa; this is *The Sarnia Observer*."

"My Grandma Martha lives in Sarnia, that's where my mom was born," I said. *Could this be my grandmother's kitchen?*

"How old is your mom?" Sam asked. "Was she alive in '83?"

"I think so. Um, she would have been five or six," I answered.

"Is this her house? Does it look familiar?" Alisha questioned.

"I don't know. I've never seen the house she grew up in. My grandmother lives in a condo now."

Suddenly, the air pressure in the room shifted. The door burst ajar, revealing a menacing shadow. The dim winter light silhouetted a towering figure moving forcefully through the doorway.

Instinctively, we huddled together, holding our breath. We stayed still, waiting to see what would happen next. It was then I noticed something ominous.

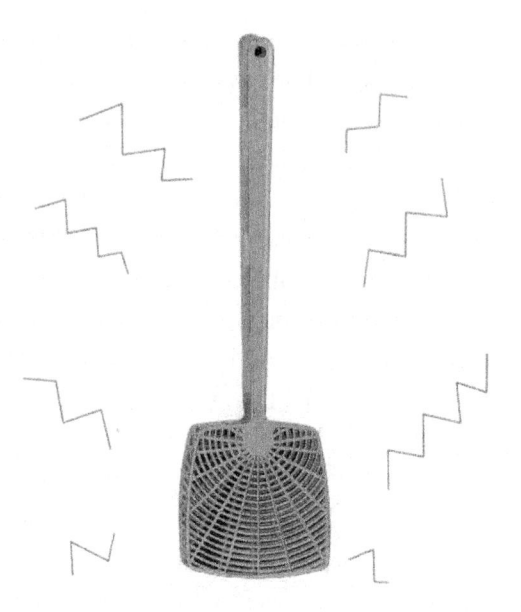

Hanging by the door, mere inches from the figure's shoulder, was a flyswatter.

5

VIEW FROM ABOVE

SLAMMING THE DOOR SHUT, a large burly man strode in with a sour look on his face. Shrugging off his coat, he tossed it onto a chair and grabbed a bottle of beer from the fridge. He took a long thirsty swig and stomped out of the room. Paralyzed by the sight of the flyswatter, I stayed stock-still, not moving even an antenna until I heard the heavy footsteps fade away.

Sam and I blurted out solutions to our shared predicament. "We have to hide," he whispered, as I said, "Let's get out of here."

Alisha, while certainly scared, was thinking clearly. "We need to keep quiet while humans are around, our buzzing will draw them to our location. Let's stick together and out of sight."

"Should be easy—there are lots of hiding places in this mess," Sam observed.

"How about on top of the cupboards?" Alisha suggested.

"Yeah, we'll have a good view from there, but no one will see us," I said. "Let's go."

We landed atop the corner cupboard when the doors opened again. This time, two people entered the room. A bleach blonde woman carrying large paper grocery bags, followed by a small girl with long straight sandy hair.

As the woman moved closer, I recognized her as a younger version of my grandmother, and saw she was fuming.

"Get a move on and clear that table! There's nowhere for me to put these bags!" she shouted at the girl.

The girl filled her little arms, obediently moving the papers. As she peered over the stack, searching for a place to put them, she lost her grasp, and they fluttered to the ground.

This further angered my grandmother. "Jennifer Ann, I asked you to clear space, not make an even bigger mess."

It was my mother! I hadn't recognized her, having never seen a picture of her as a child. She looked nothing like me, but I have been told I take after my father's side.

"Put the groceries away, clean up this mess and start dinner," she barked at my mom. "I'll be resting, so keep the racket down."

After getting a beer from the fridge, she left the kitchen. *Did she really expect such a young child to do all this herself?* We watched in astonishment as little Jennifer Ann moved around the kitchen, doggedly pushing and climbing chairs to reach surfaces designed for adults.

Sam whispered, "That's your mom, right?"

I nodded, still trying to keep quiet. "She doesn't seem

to be able to hear us from there," Alisha observed. "Just in case, let's whisper."

After emptying the bags and clearing a small space on the counter, she heated a can of tomato soup and made three ham and cheese sandwiches. She worked diligently, unaware of her observers, until a gravelly male voice bellowed from down the hall. "My dinner ready yet? I'm starving!"

"Almost, Daddy," she replied. I was having trouble connecting the child in front of me to the mother I knew. *Who was this Daddy?* Her father had died when she was an infant and my grandmother had raised her alone.

She carefully ladled the soup into bowls, bringing them one at a time to the table. Returning for the sandwiches and trying to carry them all at once, she lost her balance and one slid off its plate. As it sailed through the air, it split open, and its contents scattered across the grimy floor.

Keeping her eyes on the doorway, she put the plates back on the counter. Hands trembling, she peeled the soiled meat and cheese off the ground, wiping the slices against her dress. Putting the reassembled sandwich back on the plate, she brought it to the table and stood for a moment as though trying to decide where to place it. Hearing the sounds of footsteps approaching, she chose a spot and scurried back to retrieve the other sandwiches as the adults returned to the kitchen.

"Are those your grandparents?" Sam asked.

I hesitated to respond, however they were not looking in our direction. "That's my Grandma Martha, but I don't know who the man is. My grandfather died when my mom was a baby."

We soon learned his name as my grandmother crossly reprimanded my mother. "Jennifer Ann, where are the drinks? You know Frank and I have beer with dinner."

As my mother opened the fridge to retrieve beverages, Alisha commented, "Looks like Frank is your grandmother's boyfriend."

They sat at the table, Frank settling into the spot with the soiled sandwich. Frank and my grandmother spoke only to one another, ignoring my mom completely. When they were done, they got up and left the kitchen, pausing only to retrieve more beers.

My mother sat, finishing her meal alone, accompanied only by the hockey commentators' play-by-play emanating from the living room TV.

"Wow," said Alisha. "Maybe this is why your mom never says much."

"Yeah, force of habit," added Sam.

I didn't reply. I felt extremely sorry for her. She was so young and was being treated like a servant. I realized that my mom invisibly took care of everything at our house too. My dad helped, but it was mostly her. Feeling a new appreciation for her and everything she did, I decided to help out more, and even initiate conversations. I'd ask about her childhood and hear about what I was witnessing from her point of view.

We watched as she rose from her chair and cleaned. She cleared the table, then pulling a chair to the sink, tackled the dishes. She was squirting dish soap into the water when there was a soft tapping at the door.

My mother perked up at the sound. Hopping off the chair she ran to open the door where she greeted an old woman holding a small red tin. "Mrs. Williams! Hello, please come in," my mother said, for the first time looking and sounding like a happy child.

"Good evening, Jenny," the woman said, removing her shoes. "I made your favourite: a fresh batch of my home-made peanut butter cookies." She removed the lid and the delicious aroma wafted up to our perch.

The smell was alluring. Though I didn't have a nose, I could detect the odour through my antennae. My senses were amplified. My wings began beating, finding myself lifting off, I had to force myself back down. The same thing was happening to Sam and Alisha. They were drifting away from me, towards the cookies, and that flyswatter!

6

GRIZELDA'S COOKIES

"S<small>AM</small>! L<small>ISH</small>! C<small>OME BACK</small>!" I yelled, but they either couldn't hear, or were ignoring me. I too felt drawn by the smell, and struggled to keep my bearings.

I flew down to block their descent. "Guys, stop! It's too dangerous!" I cried.

Alisha snapped out of it and joined my efforts to stop Sam, but he was too far gone. If flies could salivate he'd have been drooling.

As he continued towards the open tin, I realized I could see the smell wafting in the air. He was picking up speed, and we had to act fast. "I have an idea. Follow me," I called to Alisha.

Dashing ahead of Sam, we cut in front of his path, intercepting the jet of cookie fragrance. "Beat your wings as fast as you can," I instructed. Frantically, we began flapping in place, dispersing the stream. It was working; the smell was still there, but not as concentrated.

I shot straight at Sam, forcing him off course. His eyes were foggy with craving, but my game of chicken worked.

Forced to dodge me, I hoped this brief interruption was enough to break the spell.

Alisha rounded on him, jostling him back to the cupboards, where we tackled him, pinning him down for his own safety.

"Aww guys, they smell so good. I want to get a closer look," he pleaded.

"No, Sam, it's not worth the risk. We just got here, I don't want you to get swatted," Alisha reasoned.

I wondered if the commotion had alerted them to our hiding spot. They had definitely noticed, and were discussing us. "Flies? In January?" the woman questioned, looking perplexed.

"Momma says I'm not doing a good job keeping this kitchen clean, so I suppose it's my fault," my mother replied, hanging her head and returning to her chair at the sink.

"Oh honey, you're doing an amazing job for such a little thing," she said, her voice brimming with compassion. "Here, you take a break and let me give you a hand. Have a cookie, Jenny. But first, bring some to the adults."

My mother divided the cookies onto two plates, one of which she took to the other room. The woman began washing dishes. Clucking softly under her breath, we heard her murmur, "Poor sweet child. She deserves better." I agreed.

Still holding onto Sam, we watched as my mom came back in and resumed cleaning. Taking the dish from her hands, the woman said, "No, no, sweetie, enjoy your cookies. I'll take care of all of this."

Thanking her profusely, she sat to enjoy her dessert, slowly nibbling her cookie until it disappeared. Finished cleaning, Mrs. Williams joined her at the table. She pushed the plate towards my mother, "Jenny, have some more. I have plenty at home."

"Thank you, Mrs. Williams," she said, reaching for another.

She was munching away happily when my grandmother came in from the living room. "Thanks for the cookies, they were delicious, as always."

"My pleasure Martha, you know I love having an excuse to visit with little Jenny."

"You're welcome anytime. It's a real treat having a neighbour who is such a good baker."

Retrieving two more bottles from the fridge, she

added, "Looks as though you cleaned up quickly tonight, Jennifer Ann. Finish your cookie and get yourself to bed. No staying up late."

"Yes, Mummy," said my mother.

As my grandmother staggered from the room, she looked back over her shoulder and said, "Have a nice evening, Grizelda."

7

WRATH OF THE FLYSWATTER

GRIZELDA? Did my grandmother know I was here? How did she know my name? I hadn't even been born yet. Sam and Alisha were confused too.

"Did she say your name?" asked Alisha.

"How does she know about you?" questioned Sam. "You guys can let me go now," he added. "The cookies are gone."

We released Sam and watched as Mrs. Williams rose. She gave my mom a hug goodbye, and holding her now empty tin, left the way she came. After the door closed, my mom rinsed off the cookie plate and turned off the lights.

We weren't in complete darkness. The light from the hall shone in to cast a soft glow into the now deserted kitchen. We heard her walking down the hall and sat quietly with our thoughts, until together, we came to the same conclusion.

Breaking the silence, though we all spoke at once, it was Sam who could be heard clearly. "It's her! She was talking to her—Mrs. Williams," he announced, bouncing up and down.

"Grizelda Williams, that's who I was named for," I said.

Alisha nodded in agreement, "She's so nice. Maybe she was the only person who was kind to your mom."

"Did your mom ever mention her?" Sam asked.

"No, my mom has never told me about her childhood. She and my grandmother don't talk much. I thought it was because my mom isn't much of a talker. Maybe it's more than that," I said.

"I'd say it is," said Alisha. "The way she treated her. Like a servant. She only spoke to her to tell her what to do, she's ignoring her daughter and spending all her time with Frank."

"So, we got the answer to our question," I said. "Why are we still here? I thought we'd pop back into our bodies when we got the answer."

"Probably because we need to sample those peanut butter cookies. There must be some crumbs. I think a crumb would be a good treat for a fly," said Sam, who, boy or fly, was always thinking about food.

"They did smell good. Let's go down and see," said Alisha.

It seemed safe enough. The kitchen was dark and empty, and those cookies did smell delicious.

"Alright," I agreed, "but let's bring them back up here to eat." I felt safer up in our little perch.

We flew down, and sure enough, the floor was littered with cookie crumbs and more. The floor had not been swept for some time, it was a veritable fly feast.

Overlooking the fact that I was about to eat garbage

off a filthy floor, I zeroed in on a sweet-smelling cookie crumb. Though I could manoeuvre the food with my stick arms, picking anything up was impossible and I soon abandoned my idea of bringing the food back up to our perch. It's not like anyone was in the room to catch us.

Using our tube-shaped mouth pieces, which, I later learned are called *proboscises*, we began feasting.

Fortunately, we didn't need to know the term proboscis in order to use them, nor did we need to know how flies eat, to eat. Much like flying, instincts kicked in. It's a good thing too—had I known what I was doing, I might have been too grossed out to enjoy my cookie crumb.

A fly's proboscis acts like a sponge, soaking up liquid. Cookie crumbs are not liquid, but solid, and this is where it gets really icky.

To eat a solid, a fly, or in this case, yours truly, regurgitates onto the food. Regurgitate is a fancy word for puke, vomit, throw-up, tossing your cookies. Yep, to eat our cookies, we tossed onto them first.

The vomit contains digestive juices, which breaks the food apart, liquefying it and turning it into proboscis-ready delights. It differed greatly from how we ate as humans, but was delicious nonetheless.

How we tasted food also differed. Our taste buds were tiny hairs on the ends of our legs, called *tarsi*. It was a very unique experience, tasting with our feet instead of our tongues. We got to taste before eating.

"Ah, so good!" Sam was voraciously gobbling up, vomit-soaked cookie crumbs.

"Uh huh," mumbled Alisha, focusing on the soggy cookies. The pair resembled winged vacuums with legs.

My cookie crumb finished, I looked for another morsel to sample. I found what appeared to be a giant doughnut, but was actually a piece of cereal.

Before I could bring myself to touch it, I involuntarily began rubbing my hands together. I was compelled to remove every minute fragment of cookie before moving on to the next item. When I finally deemed my hands clean, I moved on to my eyes and my face. I had to rub everywhere before I could taste the next thing.

"Griz, what are you doing?" asked Alisha, who then began moving through the motions of the very same routine. "Wait, what am I doing? I... I can't stop!"

"I've always wondered why flies rub their hands together like plotting super-villains," I said, after completing my spontaneous performance, "It's getting clean."

Sam stopped gorging long enough to take us in and the next thing we knew, he had joined us in our cleaning regimen.

"So, that's why flies do that. No soap for us flies, we have to rub it away," said Sam, vigorously rubbing his eyes. "Hey, here's one for you. A time traveller walks into a restaurant. He enjoyed his food so much he went back **four** seconds."

"Good one Sam, tell Griz the one about the..." said Alisha. She was about to say more, but was cut short by the dim hum that proceeded the flickering of the fluorescent lights.

Frank had entered the room. We stayed still, hiding in

plain sight, praying he did not spot us as he made his way to the fridge.

He opened it without so much as a glance in our direction, retrieved two beers and headed back the way he came. He was reaching for the light switch when he stopped in his tracks.

"Pretzels," he muttered. He spun on his heels and stumbled straight towards us.

As his footsteps approached, we had to make a quick decision. Either stay where we were, and trust he wouldn't step on us, or make a run for it and hope he didn't notice us flying away.

There was something about being a fly that worked to our advantage. I didn't understand it at the time, but Alisha read about it after our return. It explained what occurred next.

Scientists have observed that time passes more slowly for insects, or at least their perception of it differs from ours. Something that feels fast for a human, such as a newspaper swatting through the air, moves in slow motion for a fly. It gives us flies more time to react and plan our next moves. That was what happened as Frank's foot was coming in to smoosh us. Though he was walking fast, we had ample time to manoeuvre out of harm's way.

"Go straight up!" Alisha cried.

As we flew out of danger, her buzzing, combined with the trajectory of our flight path brought Frank's attention to our presence.

"Dang flies!" he cussed, swinging his arms, hands still holding tight to his drinks. A bottle barely missed Sam, passing so near I could see foamy bubbles forming beneath the brown glass of the stubby bottle.

He put the beers on the counter and headed towards the flyswatter. We had to get out of the kitchen and fast.

"Follow me," I buzzed, and we sped off into the darkness.

As we made our escape, we heard Frank calling out behind us. "Martha, you got flies in here! Flies in January!"

8

PLAYING SMALL

FLYING through the darkened hall in tight formation was exhilarating. We had escaped. This was fun. I felt a little scared, but more brave than fearful. It was liberating, knowing capture merely meant returning to our normal lives. We weren't done here yet, and instinctively avoided death. But I wasn't frightened the way I would have been if this were happening in my human form.

"Where to now?" Sam asked. This being my grand-mother's house, it seemed I was in charge of our itinerary.

"I've never been here before," I replied. "But I think we're better off choosing an empty room."

"Not the living room, then," announced Alisha, as we passed the blurry outline of my grandmother reclining on an olive-green couch, her feet propped on a matching ottoman.

There were three other doorways to choose from. One, with a slit of light shining through the gap where the closed door met the floor. The others dark, with doors ajar.

Drawn by the dull light that filtered through the thin fabric of the curtained window, I chose the open one on the right. We circled behind the material, landing on the frigid dusty sill.

The room wasn't dark for long, someone entered and turned on the light. Certain Frank had pursued us, I pictured him hunting us tenaciously, armed with that dreadful red flyswatter.

We heard a soft humming that could only come from a young girl—in this case my mother—and let out a collective sigh of relief. Feeling emboldened by the room's occupant being a child, rather than an angry man, Sam dared to fly out and peek around the curtain.

"It's Jenny, she's playing. We're safe."

Jenny? Playing? This still felt so weird. Not only our being flies, but my mom, so young and innocent. I had never thought of her as a child before. I mean, I know she was one, but all I could ever picture was a smaller version of the woman I knew. *Playing?* No. The mental image of the miniature adult playing had never occurred. That was too much of a stretch, it didn't fit with her. Play was not a setting the mother I knew possessed. I had to see it to believe it. The girl working somberly in the kitchen couldn't be my only memory of her upon my return to normal life.

"I have to see this," I said to my friends. They both followed as I lifted off the sill. We circled around the curtain and I spotted a tall wooden dresser in the corner. Soundlessly, we crossed the room and surveyed the top. We landed inside an open jewellery box, shielding ourselves from view behind the ballerina emerging from the centre.

Donning a minuscule pink tutu and standing forever at attention on pointed toe, we joined this tiny dancer at her post. Her arms arched gracefully, I imagined her keeping watch over my mother, patiently awaiting the music, her cue to twirl in slow melodic circles.

There, alongside the stoic ballerina, we observed as Jenny, now ready for bed in a blue checkered flannel nightgown, played alone. She had toys and dolls, and we watched as she brought them to life, constructing elaborate stories for them to act out. She played happily, entertaining herself, and us as well. A spell was cast wherein we forgot the surly adults down the hall—that was until they came to her door.

As the pair stood in the doorway looking nonplussed, Frank slung his arm possessively over my grandmother's shoulder.

"Jennifer Ann," launched my grandmother in a tone that could only be followed by a reprimand, "It's well past your bedtime. Get yourself straight to bed," she said, slurring her last few words.

"Yes, Momma. I'm sorry. I'll be just a minute," replied my mother, keeping her head down, focused on the dolls before her.

What came next shocked us, but apparently not her. Frank exploded in a bout of rage, pushing in front of my grandmother. Hands on hips, he bent at the waist until his fuming face was mere inches from my mother's bowed head.

"You'd best respect your mother in front of me, young lady. When she done tell you to get to bed you better get! No excuses and no 'one more minute' business, missy!"

Face red as a tomato, spitting as he spoke, he thundered on. "Since you think you know better than us, tell me what is so dang important that you need one more minute?"

Not daring to look up, she whispered, "I was going to put my toys away, sir."

Now it was my grandmother's turn to be incensed. "Sir? Now, Jennifer Ann I told you Frank and I are getting married. You call him Daddy like I said!"

"Sorry, Momma. I'll put my toys away now, Daddy."

Mildly appeased, Frank said, "Now that's a good girl, you get right to bed once you're done."

They didn't stay to ensure her obedience, nor to wish her goodnight. They merely turned and staggered into the room across the hall.

Clutching a doll in her arms, she placed everything

else in her toy chest and climbed into bed before extinguishing the lamp on the night table. The pitch black reflected the pit I felt in my stomach. For all my complaints about my mother's lack of attention, what she had lived through was an entirely different matter.

She always kissed me goodnight. When she did speak, it was always kind. She didn't make me cook and clean like a slave, and she didn't bring home mean men and make me call them Daddy. I began to see Jennifer Ann as a person. Not only a mother, nor a little girl, but all those things and more wrapped into one.

I felt like I could cry. Then, I heard her. She wasn't crying. She was singing. A soft lullaby I recalled from my younger days. Listening to it softened my grief. I thought about all she had overcome, having had this kind of upbringing and managing to give me so much more. I vowed to appreciate her, to give and receive more love and attention. To learn from this, and to someday be fully present for my own children. To give them what my mother and I had lacked. I imagined each generation, improving upon the last, enriching the next.

My eyes adjusted to the absence of light in the room. I could make out the silhouettes of Sam, Alisha, the ballerina, and the small slender shape of my mother under her covers. I was about to share my thoughts with Sam and Alisha but before I could get the words out, her lullaby ended. My mother, holding her doll in outstretched arms, spoke soothingly.

"Grizelda, that's what I name you. Mrs. Williams would be a good mommy. I am your mommy. I will call you Grizelda and I will be Mrs. Williams. I will make you

cookies every day and love you and care for you always."
She hugged the doll tightly, then turned over to sleep.

With that, we were back in our bodies. Back in the
school yard, back in Ottawa. Back to our place and time.

9

RETURN TRIP

YOU'D THINK after such an experience we'd be excited. Jumping around, kissing the ground or maybe our human non-fly bodies. You'd think we'd be screaming, talking a mile a minute. Reliving every detail about our journey, comparing notes. You'd be wrong. Yes, we did later meticulously discuss and document every moment as flies. But not right then, not right there.

Instead, with blank expressions, the three of us stood staring at one another, attempting to process what had happened. Then, we plopped down on the grass, sitting in heavy silence as our oblivious schoolmates played around us. Alisha pulled fistfuls of grass and Sam toyed with his shoelaces. We sat there until the bell rang, at which point we returned robotically to our classrooms. The rest of the day flew by. I drifted through the motions. I tried to distract myself by focusing on the lesson, rather than deciphering the journey I had undertaken.

After school, we walked with a group of kids headed the same direction and let them do the talking. It wasn't until we parted ways with the other kids that we were ready to broach the subject.

It was Sam who initiated the conversation, "Did that really happen?" he asked, stopping in his tracks.

"It did," Alisha said.

I nodded. It did.

"Just to make sure we remember the same thing... we were flies, right?" he probed further.

"Yes, in Sarnia, in the '80s," added Alisha.

"And, we saw my mom, my grandmother, and some dude named Frank," I confirmed.

"Your poor mom," said Alisha sadly.

"Yeah, it makes me see her differently," said Sam.

"Me too." I then shared my epiphany, the striking realization I had experienced prior to our departure. How I had seen my mother for who she was, and what she had lived through, and vowed to appreciate her.

"Wow, that's powerful stuff," said Alisha, rubbing my back.

Sam, lightening the mood, said, "I was going to tell a joke about time travel but nobody laughed."

We didn't laugh, we groaned. Then returning to the subject, Sam said, "That might be why we left then."

"Huh? What do you mean?" I asked.

"We asked a question about your name, and well, we got the answer when we heard your grandmother talking to the neighbour," Sam explained.

"Right," said Alisha, nodding. "We learned that you were named after Mrs. Williams when we were in the kitchen. Then, it was confirmed when we heard your mom talking to her doll. I thought that's what sent us back, but maybe it wasn't only about getting the answer.

Maybe it was the feelings you felt. The agreement you made with yourself. Maybe that's what ended our time travel as flies."

I thought about what they were saying, it was true. I had felt bad for my mom in the kitchen when we learned Mrs. Williams' first name; but it wasn't until we were in the bedroom, watching her being neglected and treated so poorly that I felt true compassion.

"Well," I said, "that may be what triggered it. All I know is I love my mom and I forgive her for overlooking me. So, to connect with her I'm going to do more talking, I'm going to start by asking about her childhood."

"Good idea," said Alisha, as we began walking again.

"Yeah, try to find out whatever happened to that tool Frank," said Sam. "They never did get married, right?"

"Nope, at least I don't think so…" There was so much for me to find out.

As we climbed the front steps to the Summers' house, Sam asked the question I thought would have been the first from his mouth. "So, you guys ready for our next trip?"

Alisha shook her head vehemently. "No way, I need time back here in my lovely house as my lovely self before I'm ready to do that again."

"I agree 1000%," I said.

As Sam opened the door, he turned and smiled that mischievous smile, "Great. You're up for doing it again. I'll get the list."

He kicked off his shoes and was running down the hall before we could respond. Alisha and I looked at one another and I had to laugh when she said, "Wait until you see the size of this list."

10

KITCHEN CONVERSATIONS

THAT EVENING, when my mom picked me up, I ran into her arms and gave her the biggest bear hug ever. "Grizelda, it's good to see you too," she said, surprised.

"How was your day, Mom? Did you have fun? What did you have for lunch? Did you have any sweets? Tell me all about it," I asked rapid-fire, then stopped, awaiting her response.

Amused, she smiled at the Summerses. Then, she bent to my level and replied, "I had fun. I ate soup and a sandwich and a cookie for dessert. C'mon, I'll tell you about my day and you tell me about yours. OK, sweetheart?"

"Sure Mom, I'll tell you *all* about my day," I said. Winking at Sam and Alisha, I added, "at school." Holding back laughter, we struggled to keep straight faces as I departed.

That night my dad worked late, so Mom and I spent a long time talking. On the drive home, we talked about our days (I omitted the time travel part), then at home, in the kitchen, we talked about her childhood.

As I helped peel vegetables, I bombarded her with questions. My line of inquiry became more direct after my initial, too subtle queries failed to jog her memory. Once she started talking, she opened up and shared intimate details about her childhood. I learned about my grandmother, her ongoing alcoholism, her nasty temper, and of Frank. One of the many men who had come in and out of their lives. They weren't all mean, but she had to call them all Daddy, which she found very confusing.

When I asked her if she'd had any positive role models, we finally got to Grizelda Williams, my namesake.

"Yes Griz, I had someone," she replied, pausing her chopping and looking wistfully out the window. "My neighbour, Mrs. Williams, the most positive person I've ever known. Without her watching over me, I'm not sure I would have survived."

"What do you mean?" I prodded.

"She treated me kindly, like I was her own daughter. She taught me how to cook, how to clean and she did a lot of both of those things for me. You see, Grandma wasn't well enough to take care of herself, let alone me."

Putting the knife down on the cutting board, she turned to me, "Most importantly, she saw me, she heard me, she loved me, Griz. All things that my mother wouldn't, or couldn't, do."

Tears welled in my mother's beautiful brown eyes and I reached out to hug her. I felt like I was comforting the little girl from some thirty years ago I had watched putting herself to bed.

"Griz, I named you after her," she said, gripping me by my shoulders and kneeling beside me so we were locked eye to eye. "I promised myself the day you were born that I would treat you so well. Not how I was treated, but how Grizelda Williams would have raised her own child, had she had any."

"You do, Mom," I said.

"No sweetie, I don't. But I will," she said in a raspy voice.

"When you asked me this weekend about how I chose your name, it opened something inside me. Now, with us talking about this, I have to admit to you and myself that I'm a better mom than Grandma ever was, but, I'm not at all like Mrs. Williams. I've broken my own vow."

Though my eyes were dry, I felt a hard lump pressing painfully against my throat threatening to choke me if I dared to speak. Instead, I gulped and shook my head.

She went on, "I got so caught up in working to provide you with all the things I never had, that I forgot about what Mrs. Williams really gave me: her attention." Her voice broke and with tears streaming, she hoarsely whispered, "I'm so sorry, baby, I'll do better. I love you, Grizzy Bear."

She hadn't called me that in years, it was her pet name for me when I was little. Somewhere along the line she had stopped using it. Hearing that name, released the lump I had been straining to hold back. I coughed, sputtered and bawled like a baby as she pulled me onto her lap and together we cried until I could speak.

"I love you too, Mommy," I said, also using a name that had fallen out of use. "I understand. I forgive you."

"Thank you, sweetie," she said, "I promise, things will

be different." I knew she was right, things were already different. She was different, I was different.

As we picked ourselves up off the floor, we heard my dad come in. "Hey, I'm home. What smells so good in here?" he called.

Walking into the kitchen, he lost his balance and did a funny little sidestep. "Hey! What the..." he said, flapping his hands around his head.

"Flies, three of them. Flew right into my face," he explained.

"Oh, would you like the flyswatter?" my mom asked, wiping the remaining tears with the back of her sleeve.

"No!" I cried, taken aback.

Surprised by my strong reaction, my dad guessed, "Is this part of your vegetarianism, Griz?"

"Yeah, something like that," I replied.

"Live and let live," said my mom, pulling us into a group hug.

It felt great to be folded in their arms. As they squeezed me tight, I heard a soft buzzing coming from above.

There, perched on the top of the cabinets, were three little flies. Or three time travellers. I'll never know. I do know I'll never look at a fly, or my mother, the same way again.

Not *THE END*... just the beginning.

BONUS MATERIALS

BUG BUZZ BOOK CLUB: *Discussion Topics*
LIFE OF FLY: *Facts About Flies*
TIMEFLIES TRAVEL TRIVIA: *Story Setting Information*
BUZZWORDS: *Vocabulary Builder*

For printable versions of these bonus materials and more visit: www.motherbutterfly.com/educational-resources

BUG BUZZ BOOK CLUB

Discussion Topics

1. *In Chapter 2, Sam shows Alisha and Griz the amber cubes. Though he says one lick is enough, it is unclear what the cubes do. He also pressures Griz into agreeing to something unknown and hides the cubes from his mother. What makes this behaviour suspect in real life? Discuss the dangers of consuming unknown substances and how you would respond in this scenario.*

2. *At the end of Chapter 2, Grizelda wishes she was a Summers. In Chapter 3, her trip to Toronto is tainted by her parents' behaviour. Discuss what causes her to feel this way. Is this something you can relate*

to? Share your insights on how a child can improve communication with distracted parents.

3. In Chapter 3, to be supportive, Griz decides to keep her misgivings to herself and go along with Sam and Alisha's make-believe. Would it have been better to be honest and express her doubts? Is it appropriate to tell white lies to avoid dashing the hopes of others, or is lying always wrong? Discuss.

4. Grizelda's mother, Jennifer Ann, shoulders a heavy burden. At a young age, she is saddled with many responsibilities and is treated poorly by her mother and her mother's boyfriend. Seeing this, Griz's perception of her mother shifts from critical to appreciative. Discuss how childhood upbringing can influence future behaviours. Are we doomed to repeat history, or does seeing what we don't like give us the motivation to create something better?

5. In Chapter 7, the TIMEFLIES escape from being crushed by Frank's foot. They attribute their escape to insects perceiving time differently from humans. A study led by Dr. Andrew Jackson from Trinity College Dublin, found that flies perceive light flickering up to four times faster than

we can, thus, seeing everything in slow motion. Could time be relative rather than fixed? Is time proportionate to size? Does time fly when you're having fun? Have you ever felt time slow down or speed up? Discuss.

LIFE OF FLY

The idiom, 'To be a fly on the wall', refers to being able to observe a situation closely without interfering or being noticed. This phrase originated in America in the 1920s and the first known citation is from 1921.

> "I'd just love to be a fly on the wall when the Right Man comes along."
>
> — THE OAKLAND TRIBUNE, FEBRUARY 1921

In the TIMEFLIES series, by becoming actual *flies on the wall,* Grizelda, Alisha, and Sam observe their family histories and discover what it is like to live as a housefly. This **Life of Fly** section explores the fascinating lives of houseflies, also known as *Musca domestica*.

Life Cycle of a Housefly

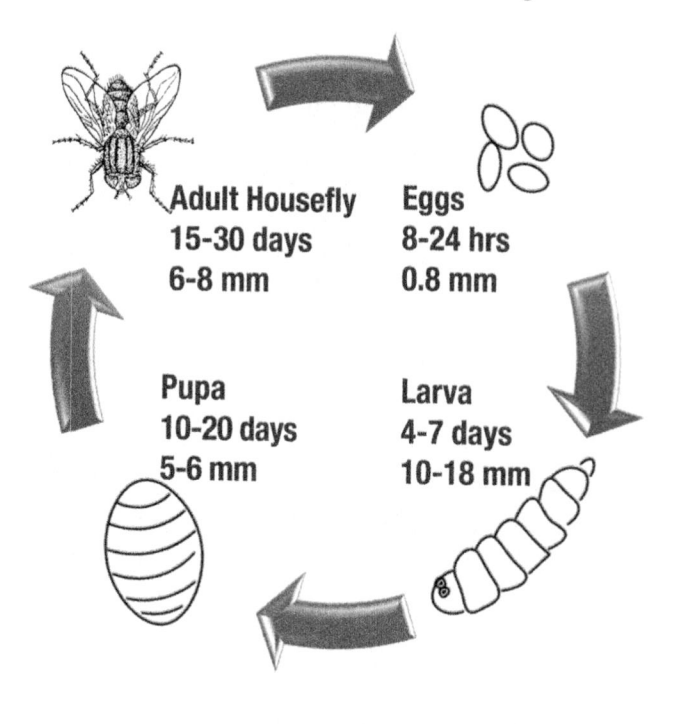

Adult Housefly
15-30 days
6-8 mm

Eggs
8-24 hrs
0.8 mm

Pupa
10-20 days
5-6 mm

Larva
4-7 days
10-18 mm

A housefly's **life expectancy** varies based upon temperature and living conditions. Flies living in warm environments develop faster and live longer than their counterparts in colder climates. Houseflies go through four stages: **egg, larva, pupa, and adult.** Their short life cycle allows them to multiply quickly.

~

Fly Anatomy

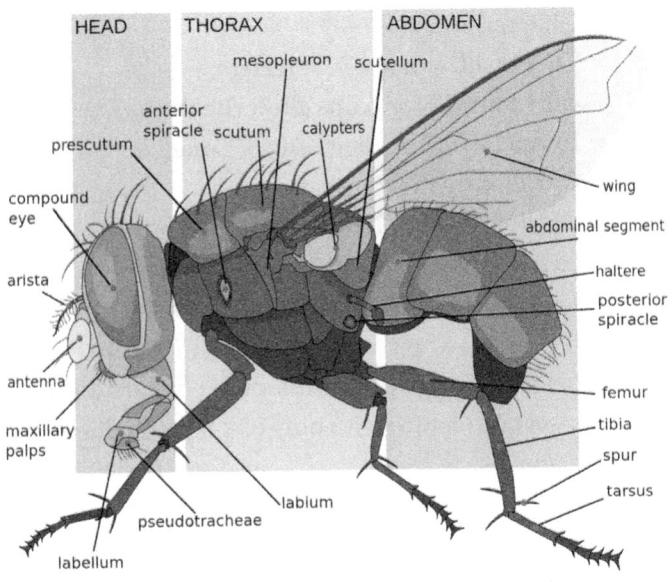

Image by Al2 edited by Muhammad Mahdi Karim via Wikimedia Commons GFDL

- Their bodies, covered with bristles, are comprised of the **head, thorax and abdomen**.
- A pair of large **compound eyes** cover most of the head. Each eye is composed of 3 to 6 thousand **simple eyes.**
- Between the two compound eyes are three additional simple eyes called **ocelli.** The ocelli act as a navigational device, letting the fly know which way is up.
- At the tip of their **proboscis** (trunk-like appendage) are the **labellum** (lips) and **pseudotracheae** (tubes) which sop up liquids

like a sponge. Salivary secretions dissolve and collect food particles as described in Chapter 7.

- Two small, antenna-like feelers called **maxillary palps** allow the fly to taste.
- Instead of noses, their sense of smell is provided by their antennae.
- The mid-section is of its body, the **thorax**, contains all of its limbs used for movement.
- Flies have two sets of wings. The smaller secondary wings, called **halters**, are located below the main pair. Without the halters the insect cannot fly; with only one halter, it flies in circles.
- As the TIMEFLIES ate cookie crumbs in Chapter 7, they used their legs to taste. Tiny hairs on the end leg segment, **tarsus** (plural **tarsi**), work similarly to human taste buds.
- They have claws and padded feet with moist suction pads called **pulvilli**, allowing flies to land almost anywhere.
- The final segment, the **abdomen**, contains the organs.

∼

Do Flies Spread Disease?

Yes. Not the TIMEFLIES, of course, but the common housefly is known to carry over 100 diseases, including typhoid, tuberculosis, dysentry and cholera. A serious health hazard, especially in areas with poor sanitary conditions, they transmit diseases by feeding and carrying pathogens. Their pukey eating style, as described in Chapter 7, combined with their residence of choice being garbage dumps and raw sewage, means they easily contaminate food with dangerous germs.

TIMEFLIES TRAVEL TRIVIA

In *The Maiden Voyage,* the TIMEFLIES travel to several cities. Here are some interesting facts about the places they visited: Ottawa, Sarnia, and Toronto, Ontario.

≈

OTTAWA, ONTARIO, 2018 (*GRIZ, SAM AND ALISHA'S HOME-TOWN*). LOCATED ON THE SOUTH BANK OF THE OTTAWA RIVER, IN THE EASTERN PART OF SOUTHERN ONTARIO. OTTAWA BORDERS GATINEAU, QUEBEC.

45.4215° N, 75.6972° W

- Chosen by Queen Victoria in 1857 to be the **capital city of Canada.**
- Ottawa is the **4th largest city** in Canada.
- Opened in 1832, the **Rideau Canal, a UNESCO World Heritage Site,** connects Ottawa to Lake

Ontario and the Saint Lawrence River. In winter, a 7.8-kilometer section in central Ottawa is cleared to become the **world's largest skating rink.**

- From the 1930s to 2013, Parliament Hill was the home to the **Canadian Parliamentary Cats.** A colony of over 30 cats lived in a sanctuary behind the Hill. Originally brought in as a natural solution to deal with rats and mice they remained for years with caregivers tending to their wellbeing.
- Visitors can **stay in a hostel** that was a **nineteenth-century jail.**
- Almost half the population is under the age of 35, making Ottawa one of the **youngest cities in the country.**
- With the most scientists, engineers and PhDs per capita, Ottawa is ranked as the **most educated Canadian city.** Continually rated as the **best place to live in Canada**, it placed 2nd nationally and 24th worldwide in the 2017 quality of life index.

~

SARNIA, ONTARIO, 1983 (*GRIZELDA'S MOTHER'S HOMETOWN*). LOCATED ON THE EASTERN SHORE OF LAKE HURON, AT THE MOUTH OF ST. CLAIRE RIVER, WHICH FORMS THE CANADA-UNITED STATES BORDER. SARNIA IS DIRECTLY ACROSS FROM PORT HURON, MICHIGAN.

42.9745° N, 82.4066° W

- Hometown of **Chris Hadfield**, the first Canadian astronaut to walk, and to record a song, in space.
- First Nations people have lived in the area for at least 10,000 years. The Midewiwin birch bark scrolls show the **Three Fires Confederacy**, a long-standing alliance of the Ojibwa, Odawa and Potowatami clans, was formed about A.D. 796. By the 1700s, the Confederacy governed an autonomous society in the hub of the great lakes, including Sarnia.
- A 40-square-kilometre area south of downtown Sarnia, known as **Chemical Valley**, is home to more than 60 chemical plants and oil refineries. Operating day and night, with toxic air billowing from smokestacks, there are 57 facilities registered as polluters within 25 kilometres of Sarnia.
- **Warning Sirens** alert residents to seek shelter indoors and tune to local radio stations in case of chemical emergencies. Siren testing can be heard every Monday at 12:30pm.

❧

TORONTO, ONTARIO, 2018 (*WEEKEND VACATION SPOT FOR GRIZELDA AND HER PARENTS*). LOCATED IN SOUTHERN ONTARIO ALONG LAKE ONTARIO'S NORTHWESTERN SHORE.
43.6532° N, 79.3832° W

- The **capital** of the province of **Ontario**,

- **Largest city in Canada** and 4th largest in North America by population.
- Originally named **York, the capital of Upper Canada** in 1793; it was incorporated and renamed Toronto in 1834.
- Rated as the world's **4th most livable city.**
- Home to over 16,000 animals representing 491 species, the **Toronto Zoo is the largest in Canada.**
- Toronto Island is the **largest urban car-free community** in North America.
- Home to over 70 **film festivals,** including the Toronto International Film Festival.
- North America's **3rd largest venue for movie production,** around 25% of Hollywood movies are filmed in Toronto.
- The **CN Tower,** 1,815 feet tall, was the tallest freestanding structure in the world before 2007.
- Toronto's **Casa Loma** is the only truly authentic castle in North America.
- Almost 25% of Canada's population **lives within a 160 km radius** of Toronto.
- Toronto is the only Canadian city with representation in 7 **major league sports.**
- The Rogers Centre is the first stadium in the world to have a **fully retractable roof.**
- Toronto has the **2nd largest public transit system** in North America.

BUZZ WORDS

When recounting their adventures, the TIMEFLIES like to use BIG words.

Expand your vocabulary with these
BUZZ WORDS
& learn their definitions at:
HTTP://MOTHERBUTTERFLY.COM/EDUCATIONAL-RESOURCES

*Accustom, Ajar, Alcoholism, Allure, Amber,
Ample, Antenna, Appease, Appliance,
Appreciation, Aroma, Asylum, Bellow,
Bizarre, Bombard, Burly, Charade,
Cobbler, Commotion, Compassion,
Compel, Concede, Concentrate,
Conclusion, Console, Contemplate,
Decipher, Detect, Digestive, Diligent,
Discreet, Distort, Doggedly, Don,
Dramatic, Earshot, Elaborate, Emanate,
Embolden, Emphasize, Enriching,*

Enthusiasm, Entrant, Epic, Epiphany,
Exasperate, Exhilarate, Extinguish,
Extraordinary, Facial, Filter, Flannel,
Fluorescent, Flutter, Flyswatter,
Formation, Forthcoming, Fragment,
Frantically, Frigid, Generation,
Ginormous, Grim, Gullible, Halter, Idiom,
Illuminate, Incensed, Incredulity, Initiate,
Innate, Innocent, Instinctive, Intensity,
Intercept, Involuntary, Iridescent,
Itinerary, Jostle, Jurassic, Labellum,
Liberate, Liquefy, Littered, Lopsided,
Manoeuvre, Maxillary Palps, Meek,
Melodic, Menace, Meticulous, Metronome,
Miniature, Minuscule, Minute,
Mischievous, Misgiving, Momentum,
Morsel, Mundane, Namesake,
Nearsighted, Neglect, Nonplussed,
Obedience, Oblivious, Ocelli, Occupant,
Ominous, Omit, Ottoman, Paralyze,
Parliament, Peculiar, Perception, Perch,
Peripheral, Perplex, Pervasive, Phony,
Pique, Possessive, Predicament, Proboscis,
Profuse, Pseudotrachea, Pulvilli, Quench,
Query, Rapid-fire, Reflective, Regimen,
Regurgitate, Reluctantly, Reprimand,
Resemble, Resume, Robotic, Salivate,
Scam, Servant, Silhouette, Simultaneous,
Slurring, Soiled, Solemn, Somber,
Spontaneous, Staggered, Stock-still, Stoic,
Supportive, Surly, Surrogate, Suspend,
Swindle, Tarsi, Taunting, Tempting,

Tenacious, Theory, Towering, Trajectory, Trigger, Unison, Vegetarian, Vehement, Veritable, Vigorous, Voracious, Vow, Waft, Wistful, Witness.

KEEP ON BUZZING!

CONTINUE THE TIMEFLIES ADVENTURE WITH

FREE

GAMES, TRIVIA, TEACHER MATERIALS & MORE AT:

www.motherbutterfly.com/educational-resources

KEEP ON BUZZING!

Join the TIMEFLIES for their next adventure in the second book of the series, TIMEFLIES: Play it Again, Sam.

Fly back over 150 years to watch as Sam and Alisha's ancestors become Canadians. Set in the great outdoors, there are more than three flies buzzing about.

Scheduled for release in 2018

ABOUT THE AUTHOR

Canadian author M.C. Goldrick's stories are penned with humour and heart, engaging young readers as they learn about the world and their place within it. M.C. Goldrick's love of life infuses every tale with fun, joy, and appreciation.

∾

The **TIMEFLIES** series is geared towards middle-grade readers and the **Marvin the Imaginary 3D Monkey** books are ideal for a younger crowd. Parents and teachers, of all ages, get to enjoy both.

Find the latest M.C. Goldrick releases at:
www.motherbutterfly.com/authors/m-c-goldrick

CPSIA information can be obtained
at www.ICGtesting.com
Printed in the USA
LVOW03s0401270318
571252LV00001B/1/P